Too Old for Nonsense?

Age is a Crazy Thing.

by MaKreWe

A Short Note Before You Begin

This book has no table of contents.

Not out of carelessness, but by design.

A table of contents suggests order. Sequence. And the quiet hope that you'll read the important parts first and save the rest for later.

This book works differently. It doesn't want to be worked through. It wants to be opened.

You can start at the beginning. Or somewhere in the middle. Or on the page that happens to fall open, because books sometimes know better what fits in the moment.

If you feel slightly confused for a second: perfect.

Confusion is a very underrated training program — especially as we get older.

This book is not a guide. It's more like a walk without a fixed route.

You still arrive — just differently.

And if at some point you think, "Well, this feels unusual," then you're doing everything right.

Foreword

At some point, they show up — those sentences.

"You're too old for that."

"That's just how it's done now."

"You don't do that at your age anymore."

What's less interesting is who says them.

What's more interesting is how quickly you start believing them yourself.

This book collects moments exactly like that.

Not to judge them, but to pick them up for a second, turn them around, look at them from all sides — and check whether they're really as heavy as they pretend to be.

This isn't about manners, advice, or doing things "properly."

It's about nonsense that contains a surprising amount of truth — and truths that are much easier to live with when you can laugh at them.

Some of this will feel familiar.

Some of it may scratch a little.

Some of it you might rather not think all the way through — which is convenient, because you don't have to do that here either.

This book doesn't take aging seriously.

But it does take you seriously.

And if there's still a small question wandering around in the back of your mind — whether you might be too old for nonsense —

keep reading.

Age isn't entirely sure either.

To all parents in this world.

We grow together.

Confusion Has No Age

Confusion is not a symptom.

*It's a side effect of thinking,
feeling, and living —
sometimes all at once.*

It hits the young.

It hits the old.

*And it usually shows up right
when you were sure
everything was running
smoothly.*

Key, Where Are You?

I'm standing in front of the door, looking for my key.

In one pocket.

In the other pocket.

Back to the first pocket again, because sometimes … well, you never know.

I mentally retrace my steps. Kitchen. Living room. Bathroom. I'm just about to go back inside to look for it.

That's when I notice:

The door is open.

And the key is right there. In the lock. On the outside.

The whole time.

You stand there for a second, staring at that key as if it secretly put itself there just to see what you'd do.

And in that moment, you could start worrying. Or you choose the healthier option.

You laugh. Shake your head. And think:

"Ah. Another human moment."

This isn't a sign of age.

It's not proof of anything.

It's just life — when your mind briefly wandered off.

And honestly:

As long as you still manage to find the key again, everything is basically fine.

Key

You search for the key very thoroughly.

While it's already in the lock.

Being human — no age required.

Where Are My Damn Glasses?

I still remember a small airfield festival.

Summer evening, outdoors, music, a bit of alcohol — nothing wild. Just enough to make the world feel slightly soft around the edges.

At some point it got dark. And suddenly my sunglasses were gone.

I searched for them everywhere. On the tables, at the bar, on the ground, where I'd been standing before. I retraced my steps like it was a small police investigation. Very serious. Very committed.

Until someone finally said,

"Um ... they're on your head."

And there they were. The whole time. Right above me.

So what does that tell us?

That you don't have to be old for this.

Confusion hits just as easily when you're younger.

You don't need wrinkles, a diagnosis, or a particular life stage. A bit of tiredness, a bit of distraction — and boom.

Since then, I've been more relaxed about the glasses.

If they're on my head today and I'm looking for them, I don't think, "Oh no."

I think, "Ah. A classic."

Not everything is age.

A lot of it is simply human.

Classic

*You search for something with
great intensity.*

*While carrying it on your head
the whole time.*

Not everything is age.

A lot of it is simply human.

I Just Wanted to Quickly…

I just wanted to quickly take care of something. Just quickly. Two minutes. Three at most.

I don't know exactly what happened next, but suddenly I was in a different room, with a different thought, and no idea what the original plan had been.

I just stood there thinking, "Okay … there was something."

That used to be the moment when you'd get nervous.

These days it's more like: "Ah. There you are again. Welcome back."

You pause for a moment. Breathe. And wait to see whether the thought returns on its own.

Sometimes it does. Sometimes it doesn't.

And both are surprisingly okay.

Because honestly: If the biggest problem of the day is that you briefly lost yourself, you're actually doing pretty well.

Briefly Gone

You walk into a room and forget why.

Happens.

Carry on.

Remind Me... If You Remember

Him: "If I'm packing my things for work tomorrow evening and I'm looking for my wallet — it's already in the backpack. Can you remind me?"

I look at him. He looks at me.

There's quiet hope in that look ... and very little realism.

Me: "Sure. If I remember."

He nods, relieved.

Me — because truth insists: "Or if I can remember at all."

And then we both laughed. Properly.

Because that's the most honest kind of teamwork we can offer right now: two people trying to remind each other — while secretly hoping the backpack comes with a built-in memory upgrade.

In the end, we agreed on this:

The wallet is in the backpack. And the rest is ... trust.

Memory

Shared memory.

Team effort.

Outcome uncertain.

When the Brain Gallops Ahead

The other day, my husband tried to explain something to me. Just a normal word. Nothing dramatic.

He starts.

Says it.

Stumbles.

Second attempt.

Even more creative.

Third attempt.

Now it's practically a new invention.

I look at him, give him a little nudge in the right direction — and he laughs. That honest, unfiltered laugh that happens when you realize the brain ran ahead and the tongue didn't get the memo.

And suddenly this sentence forms in my mind:

What if the brain gallops ahead and the language center can't keep up?

That's what happens all the time.

Thoughts are fast. They're images, impulses, connections.

Language, on the other hand, is linear. Word by word. Syllable by syllable. It has to sort, choose, structure.

The brain has already crossed the finish line while the tongue is still tying its shoes.

And here's the beautiful part:

We can laugh.

Maybe we would have corrected ourselves more harshly in the past. Maybe we would have felt embarrassed. Now a glance and a grin are enough. Maturity sometimes shows itself not in flawless speech, but in relaxed stumbling.

Perhaps growing older isn't about everything running smoothly.

Perhaps it's about no longer needing to smooth everything out.

When thoughts gallop and words chase behind, that's not a flaw.

It's aliveness.

And as long as we can laugh about it, we are definitely not too old for nonsense.

Tempo

Thoughts at a gallop.

Everyday life at a walking pace.

The Wrong Button

There are moments when everything is prepared.

You thought ahead.

You planned.

You learned.

Take the coffee machine. You turn it on so it can heat up. Very deliberately. Just like always.

Five minutes later you come back, already looking forward to the first sip — press the button and turn it off.

Not because you don't know how it works.

Not because it's the first time you've ever used it. But because your finger briefly thought:

That'll be the right button.

Mission: coffee.

Result: silence.

And while you're standing there, the machine staring at you like a disappointed household appliance, your brain immediately launches the full diagnostic program:

"Am I getting old?"

"Am I unfocused?"

"Is my brain running in power-saving mode today?"

The truth, however, is much less dramatic — and much kinder:

The know-how is there. But doing something a thousand times doesn't guarantee perfection on the thousand-and-first.

You can have done something forever and still press the wrong button once.

That's not decline. That's being human.

Experience doesn't protect you from confusion.

It just makes you laugh sooner instead of yelling at yourself.

And maybe that's the real progress of getting older:

not that fewer mistakes happen, but that you stop taking them personally.

You didn't fail. You just hit reset for a moment.

The machine will heat up again. The coffee will still come. And life does too, by the way.

Maybe not always at the push of a button. But reliably enough to stay gentle.

And honestly:

If the biggest damage of the day is delayed coffee, things are actually going pretty well.

The Wrong Button

You turned on the coffee
machine five minutes ago so it
could heat up.

Then you go to make coffee —
and accidentally press "Off."

The know-how is there.

But doing something on repeat
doesn't mean perfect execution
every time.

Punching Robots (Blindfolded)

There are tasks on the internet that sound like you've accidentally stepped into a bad action movie.

"Prove you're not a robot."
Or even better: "Defeat the robot."

And there you are, just trying to quickly log in somewhere, place an order, or open a file — and suddenly you're a gladiator in the arena of pixels.

What does "defeat the robot" even mean?

It does not mean slapping your laptop (although that can be tempting). It means one of those security checks where you have to prove you're human.

Usually through pictures.

You're asked to rotate an image until it's "correct." Or click on all the traffic lights. Or bicycles. Or crosswalks. Or something that might once have been a traffic light before it was chopped into eight blurry squares.

So you're given a task where the system hopes: "A human will recognize this. A robot won't."

And that's exactly where the comedy begins.

Why does this exist?

Because the internet, unfortunately, isn't made up only of people searching for cake recipes and watching cat videos. There are also programs — bots — that abuse websites automatically: sending spam, cracking accounts, buying up tickets, flooding comments, attacking forms.

CAPTCHA (that's what this stuff is called) is basically a bouncer.

Unfortunately, it's a bouncer wearing sunglasses at night.

In my particular "defeat the robot" mission, I had to align the image on the right to match the one on the left. Sounds simple.

Problem: I couldn't even tell what it was supposed to be.

I rotated. I shifted. I adjusted.

And failed. Repeatedly.

Mission failed. Robot undefeated.

And while I'm sitting there, swearing that I've been a biological human for many years now, the internal diagnostic cascade kicks in immediately:

Either my brain has turned to mush.
Or I need an eye exam.
Or I'm about to get whiplash from all the head-shaking.

When the truth is usually much simpler:

The system isn't difficult because I'm stupid. It's difficult because it's badly designed.

"Select all images containing a traffic light."

A classic.

Hmm.

Is that a traffic light? Or a streetlamp? Or the corner of a sign? Or a traffic-light shadow? Or an artistic commentary on modern traffic ethics?

Some things are genuinely open to interpretation — which makes it deeply absurd to turn them into a "prove you're human" test.

Because what's actually happening here?

You're asked to prove that you're human ... by solving a task that makes you feel like a human who's starting to doubt themselves.

That's almost poetic.

The system exposing itself.

The joke is this: these tasks were designed to keep robots out. But the smarter robots get, the more complicated the tasks become.

And who suffers?

Not the robots. The humans.

It turns into an arms race where we are the collateral damage. And at some point you find yourself thinking, "If I fail this one, am I officially a toaster?"

Somewhere, a machine laughs quietly.

The only healthy reaction?

Shake your head. Swear briefly. Then laugh gently at yourself.

Because you are not less human just because you can't clearly distinguish a traffic light from a pile of pixels.

You're simply ... normal.

And honestly: if "defeating the robot" means staring at blurry traffic-light squares until you question your own existence — then the robot may have already won.

Not because it's smarter.

But because it annoyed you so thoroughly in five minutes that you logged out voluntarily.

Human Test: Failed

I didn't defeat the robot.

Not because I'm stupid.

Because I was hopelessly disoriented.

And yes:

whiplash from head-shaking is absolutely a reasonable diagnosis here.

Welcome to the club — people who fail at robots and are still completely sane.

Stone Age Humans with Wi-Fi

My friend and I recently found out that we're old. Fifty-four and fifty-five. Practically one step away from the fossil exhibit.

The information came from our kids, somewhere between 22 and 28 — adults with skin like a filter and memory like a Wi-Fi password they set themselves.

The look said it all:

"Wow. You must have lived without streaming."

Yes.

And we also found our way home without GPS. Survived without tutorials. And existed without influencers.

When I was 20, I thought:

At 50, you wear beige.

Now I know:

At 50, you wear whatever you want — and you have enough confidence not to debate it.

The young ones think we're from a different era.

True.

We come from the time when people actually called each other instead of sending seventeen voice messages.

We're the generation that knows:

– how to write a letter
– how to have a conversation
– and how to address a problem directly

Stone Age?

No.

Premium upgrade with experience.

And the best part? Inside, nothing feels like fifty-five.

Inside it's still:

"Who came up with this nonsense?"

The real perspective error lies somewhere else:

At 25, you think you're young.

At 55, you know you're alive.

That's a difference.

And if someone categorizes us as "old" again, I just smile and think:

"Sweetheart, I was already cool when you were still a loading bar."

Update

*And while we're supposedly
from the Stone Age,*

*we're standing in front of a
screen the very next day,*

*negotiating with a system
that's younger than our
sweatpants — and just as
stubborn.*

The Em Dash — or Why Everything Is Needlessly Complicated

Sometimes you just want to make a dash. A perfectly normal em dash. Not philosophical. Not symbolic. Just a dash that says:

there's more coming.

And suddenly you're in the middle of a ritual.

Hyphen, space, space, return.

Or two hyphens.

Or Alt + something.

Or return again, in case the first one didn't sound serious enough.

The em dash doesn't appear when you need it, but only once the system has decided that you really want it.

And while you're trying all of this, a small thought crosses your mind: "Wait a second ... this isn't my first document."

You've been writing for years. Decades. The know-how is there.

And yet here you are, negotiating with a word processor about a line.

That's the moment you slowly realize: Not everything that's difficult is deep. Some things are just unnecessarily complicated.

This runs through a surprising number of areas in modern life.

You need a password to change a password.

You have to prove you're not a robot by clicking images that look like modern art.

And you're expected to "use things easily" that clearly require an introductory seminar.

It's not that we've become dumber. The world has simply become … layered.

Layers on layers. Options, sub-options, settings for the settings.

And somewhere in between sits a human thinking: "I just wanted to do something quickly."

The em dash is a wonderful symbol for all of this. It's not a problem in itself. It's just a sign that systems sometimes forget who they're actually there for.

And then comes that small, liberating moment:

You stop questioning yourself and start gently suspecting the system.

Not angrily. Not bitterly.

More with a mild shake of the head and the thought:

"Alright then. This way."

Maybe that's one of the quiet skills that grows with time:

You don't have to understand everything.

You don't have to do everything right.

You're allowed to notice that some things are unnecessarily inflated — and draw an em dash.

Not perfect.

But fitting.

System Error

*If something takes ten steps
just to make a dash,*

it's rarely because of you.

It's usually the system.

A Password for Your Password

You just want to quickly change a password.

Nothing dramatic. Make it a bit more secure and get on with your life.

And then comes step one:

"Please enter your current password."

Okay. Fair.

Then step two:

"Please enter a new password."

Also fair.

Then step three:

"Please re-enter the new password."

Of course.

And then — as if it's the final boss fight — somewhere along the way you also get:

"Please verify your identity."

With a code sent by email. Or by text. Or via an app. Or by smoke signal, depending on the system's mood.

And at some point during all of this, you think:

I need a password

to change a password.

And I apparently need three more passwords
to prove that I'm me.

The know-how is there. I even understand why
this exists.

But sometimes it still feels like we made the front
door extra secure by building a second front door
in front of it. And then a gate. And then a fence.

And the key for that?

Naturally stored ... as a password.

In the end it usually works. Eventually. After
seven clicks, two codes, and a small identity crisis.

And you don't feel relieved.

You just feel ... done.

The password is changed. The soul too, slightly.

Proof of Existence

You want to change a password.

And end up in a legal-style hearing about your own existence.

You have to prove that you can prove yourself in order to be allowed to prove yourself at all.

Whiplash from Head-Shaking

A Global Standard for Healthy Sarcasm

Whiplash from head-shaking, by the way, is not imaginary.

Somewhere in the world, there would already be a regulation for it.

Head-Shaking Trauma (HST) — reportable from a shaking frequency of 3 Hz. Please fill out form HST-12a and attach proof of proper shaking technique.

Optional: documentation confirming that the shaking is not purely ideological, but caused by genuine despair.

You don't need a chiropractor.

You just need real life.

When Your Brain Hits the Dance Floor

You're sitting at the computer and really just want to quickly look something up.

Nothing dramatic. No rocket launches. No saving the world.

And then it happens:

A window pops up.

Big.

Red.

Urgent.

With exclamation marks that look like they've had coffee intravenously.

"ACT NOW!"

"YOUR COMPUTER IS AT RISK!"

"CALL IMMEDIATELY!"

And somewhere there's a number that sounds like it has about thirty seconds left before the internet explodes.

That's the moment your brain takes over.

Not the calm, adult brain.

The other one. The one with panic mode and an acrobatics license.

Thoughts start doing backflips:

What if …?

How bad is it …?

I have to …!

And while your head is dancing, your gut speaks up very quietly:

"This feels off."

Your gut doesn't say that for fun.

You almost click anyway.

Because "almost" is shockingly fast in moments like this.

And then there's that one second where you pause —

not because you suddenly understand everything,

but because you realize:

When something screams urgency this loudly, it usually isn't trying to help you.

It's just trying to make you hurry.

So:

pause.

Breathe.

And before your brain attempts the next
somersault, you ask for advice.

From a human.

Not from a blinking window with anger issues.

Panic Button

*When panic speeds things up,
pausing isn't wasting time.*

First check the facts.

Then listen to your gut.

*And before your brain hits the
dance floor:*

ask someone.

It's Me. I Just Need Some Money Real Quick.

You get a message that pretends to be family.

Short.

Simple.

Urgent.

"I've got a problem. I can't talk right now. Can you quickly send me some money?"

And there it is again: the internal alarm.

Because family + emergency + speed = your brain sprints onto the dance floor.

The nasty part is:

it sounds exactly like how you would help.

Immediately.

No questions.

No detours.

Except: helping is good. Being fast is a scammer's favorite setting.

So you do something completely unromantic:

You ask questions.

You call.

And not the number from the message — the number you've had all along.

If it's real, nobody is offended.

If it isn't, someone suddenly gets very quiet.

Are You Actually Real?

If it's urgent, check first.

Real family stays real — even after a call back.

Hand Your Money to the Police

Then there's the other version:

Strangers call and sound official.

Your house is at risk.

A burglary ring.

"Safeguarding valuables."

And suddenly the word "police" appears in a sentence like it's a free pass.

Same pattern: speed. Pressure. Fear.

And again, your brain tries to outrun logic.

The counter-move is unglamorous, but effective:

Hang up.

Breathe.

And call the police yourself — using an official number you already know (not the one someone just tells you).

Scammers hate it when you change the channel.

Real police don't.

Attention: Police

Official-sounding doesn't automatically mean real.

Real can handle a call back.

Panic

*When fear speeds things up,
pausing is protection.*

Check first.

Act second.

*And when someone is selling
urgency: call back using a
number you already know.*

The System

You explain a problem.

Calmly. Clearly. Politely.

The other person listens, nods with understanding, and then says the sentence that ends everything:

"Unfortunately, the system won't allow that."

The system.

No name. No face. No follow-up questions.

You nod automatically.

Not because you actually understand what, exactly, the system is against — but because "the system" sounds so final.

Almost like a law of nature.

Only later — usually at home, with no audience — the thought shows up:

Which system, exactly?

And why does it always make the decision right when nobody else feels like deciding?

System

Not everything that's called a "system" thinks for you.

Some things just prevent questions.

Authority Through Technology & Institutions

Not fraud itself.

But the automatic obedience that kicks in as soon as something sounds like:

Technology

Authority

Bank

Doctor

Office

Support

"The system"

What's happening here — quietly, but decisively:

Your brain doesn't start dancing just because of fear. It dances because we've learned:

"They know better than I do."

And that belief disables gut feeling and logic at the same time.

Examples many people recognize, but rarely name:

"The system doesn't allow that." → Oh. Okay then.

"You'll just have to go through this." → Alright.

"That's technically necessary." → I don't really get it, but fine.

"That's the regulation." → Guess I'm out of luck.

This isn't fraud.

It's outsourced thinking.

Authority

Not everything that sounds official is infallible.

Often we don't comply out of fear, but out of habit.

"They know better" replaces our own thinking faster than we realize.

When "We" Suddenly Become Immortal

It's interesting how generously the word *we* is used when it comes to sensational news.

"We are on the verge of immortality."

"Our generation will defeat aging."

"We are witnessing a medical breakthrough."

That *we* sounds wonderfully democratic. Almost like free drinks for everyone.

Unfortunately, the future is not an all-inclusive buffet.

Not everyone has the same genes.

Not everyone has the same bank account.

Not everyone lives stress-free on organic food with a personal trainer.

Not everyone can afford experimental therapies that are not even standard medicine yet.

If one participant in a study becomes biologically younger, that is fascinating. But it is not a group ticket to eternal life.

Television loves the big word.

Reality prefers the footnote.

Perhaps some people will live very long lives and remain remarkably fit. That would be wonderful.

Perhaps medicine will advance faster than we expect.

But before *we* become immortal, we might want to clarify exactly who this *we* includes.

The marathon runner with private insurance?

The shift worker with three jobs?

The retiree with chronic conditions?

The executive living in permanent stress?

Aging is not just biology. It is also life circumstance.

And maybe the real revolution is not about reaching 150. Maybe it is about making sure as many people as possible can still laugh without pain at 75.

Immortality sounds spectacular. Equitable health for many sounds less glamorous. But far more meaningful.

Until then, if someone on television says "we," it is perfectly fair to ask who exactly has been invited.

That is not cynicism. It is simply a well-maintained question mark.

Experts

Not everything that carries a title carries certainty.

Sometimes it only prevents the next question.

Not everything that is explained is settled.

Sometimes it is simply loud enough to sound like truth.

Three Euros for a Toilet Trip

At some point in life, conversations land on the table that would never have belonged there before.

For example: digestion.

A father in his eighties is fighting stubborn constipation. Pharmacy after pharmacy. Powders, sachets, hope.

On the table there's a box of little packets you dissolve in water. The mother grins and says:

"One sachet costs one euro. He should really take three — less doesn't do anything. He's tried."

Short pause.

Then the sentence:

"Three euros for one toilet trip."

And before anyone can nod with dignity, the verdict arrives:

"You're literally sh*tting your money away."

First: stunned faces.

Then: general laughter.

And that's the moment you realize:

Age might take away control of your gut.

But it doesn't necessarily take away your sense of humor.

People talk about things they used to stay quiet about. Not out of disrespect. Out of experience.

The body does what it wants.

The money goes where it has to.

And if you can laugh about it, you've already won a lot.

Because honestly:

If you can laugh at your own digestion, life hasn't beaten you.

You call things by their name. And if possible, you laugh.

Not because you don't care.

Because you've learned.

Anyone who's realized that the body has zero respect for social taboos can also say, with full dignity:

"Alright then. We'll talk about it."

You don't get more embarrassing with the years.

You get more honest.

More direct.

And sometimes funnier — because you stop taking yourself quite so seriously.

And maybe that's one of those upgrades you only learn to appreciate later.

Honest

The body doesn't follow taboos.

So why should we?

Humor helps with digestion.

In every sense.

And some money isn't gone.

It's just …

through.

Alcohol & Not Quite Tolerating It — Trying to Keep Up

Back then, it was easy.

You drank, you laughed, you went to bed — done.

Now it's different.

Not dramatic.

But long-lasting.

You know your body has different plans these days.

Not immediately — with a delay.

With headaches, exhaustion, and a very clear message the next day.

And still, there you are at the party, looking around and thinking:

Drinking water now would be … noticeable.

So you drink along.

Not because you want to.

Because it's polite.

Or habit.

Or because you're not quite ready to take yourself seriously yet.

The next day, your body takes you very seriously.

Signals from the Body

Some signals arrive late.

We still don't listen any earlier.

Herrmann Logic: Maturity Is Not a Step Back

I used to want everything immediately.

Fix it now.

Solve it now.

Decide now.

Be done now.

And if something didn't happen right away, I automatically thought:

"Then something must be wrong."

Well.

Then Herrmann entered my life.

Herrmann is a sourdough starter that looks at you from his unassuming glass jar as if to say:

"You can feed me — but you can't rush me."

You can't force Herrmann to mature.

You can't motivate him.

You can't "just quickly" make him perfect because you're in a hurry.

Herrmann has his own plan.

You feed him.

You put him down.

You walk away.

And while you're busy living your life, he does … his thing. And at some point, without any drama at all, he's suddenly just right. That's when I understood:

Some things in life aren't slow because they're wrong.

Some things are slow because they need time to mature.

And that's one of the advantages of getting older:

At some point, you lose the reflex to overthink everything and push it to death.

You can let things sit for a while without the internal alarm system going off.

You don't become sluggish.

You become smarter about timing.

And that's exactly why maturity isn't a step back.

It's Herrmann logic.

Herrmann Tells Us:

I don't need to become faster.

I just need to let things mature with patience.

Herrmann is proof:

Pressure doesn't make things better — just stickier.

Velcro Is Hard-Earned End Level

My husband has decided that from now on, he only wants shoes with Velcro.

I looked at him, and before I could even think, it came out of my mouth:

"Sure. That's how it starts with kids — and how it ends in old age."

He sat there trying to tie his shoes ... and his face turned bright red.

I asked if he was about to explode.

And then it happened:

We had one of those laughing fits. The kind you can't stop, because it's both so ridiculous and so true.

That kind of laughter that isn't about someone — it's with life.

And honestly:

Tying shoes is sometimes worse than a full workout.

Especially when you realize your body suddenly has priorities that don't include your pride.

So there we were:

A man nearly launching into orbit just from tying laces.

And me barely holding it together from laughing.

And that's the real message:

Humor makes everything more bearable.

Not because it magically removes problems.

But because it loosens them.

Because it reminds you:

"You're not broken. You're just in a new chapter."

As a kid, Velcro is pure freedom. You can run off without needing a certification in loop physics.

And years later, you end up right back there.

Not because you're "old."

But because you're no longer interested in being emotionally challenged by a piece of string.

So you simply say:

"I'm saving my energy for things that actually matter."

Velcro isn't surrender.

Velcro is a decision.

And if you ask me:

That's not a step back.

That's end level.

Age doesn't take things from you.

It gives you permission to make life easier.

Continuing, with Detours

You can find new paths.

Detours aren't failure.

They're experience in motion.

Are You Seriously Asking Me This Right Now?

You're doing something completely normal on your phone or computer.

Nothing wild. No drama. Just click, done.

And suddenly a question pops up:

"Do you like this ...?"

You stare at it. Read it again. And think:

Do I like ... what, exactly?

You just wanted to confirm something quickly. Instead, it feels like a program is trying to emotionally connect with you right in the middle of your day.

For three seconds, you're thrown off. Tripped up by a question that pretends to be bigger than it is.

And then it dawns on you:

This isn't a deep conversation.

It's just a pop-up. A little window pretending to be important.

You click something. Because you want to move on. Not because you've genuinely resolved the question.

And as you click it away, you think:

"Honestly ... I just wanted to continue.

Not evaluate my life."

Pop-Up Question

You just wanted to click through quickly.

What you got instead was unnecessary nonsense.

Nobody really needs that.

"At My Age..."

"At my age, you just don't do that anymore."

"At my age, you can't expect that."

"At my age, that's just how it is."

The sentence sounds harmless. Almost reasonable. And it's surprisingly useful.

Because "at my age" can end anything. Discussions. Hopes. Curiosity. Sometimes even yourself.

But the sentence is rarely a fact.

It's more like a shield. A well-meant one.

It protects you from disappointment. From effort. From the risk that something might still be possible.

And yes — some things really don't work the way they used to. That's no secret.

But surprisingly often, the sentence gets used before anyone has even checked what might still work in a different way.

"At my age ..." is sometimes not an ending.

It's an early exit.

And the tricky part is: no one argues. Because it sounds "realistic."

But realism isn't the same thing as limiting yourself.

Sometimes a more honest version would be:

"I don't feel like it right now."

"I don't feel confident about that at the moment."

Or simply: "Not today."

That leaves the door open. For tomorrow. Or the day after. Or for a different version of it.

"At my age …" doesn't have to be a full stop.

It can just be a pause.

Excuse

"At my age ..."

is often not a fact.

It's a shield.

The Self-Sewn Straitjacket

You have wishes.

Ideas.

Thoughts that are actually quite clear.

Before you act on them, the next question reliably shows up:

What might others say about this?

You run through the possible reactions.

Very thoroughly.

And in the end, you choose the safest option:

Better not.

That feels sensible. Mature. And pleasantly conflict-free.

Until you realize that in the process, you've very neatly edited yourself out.

Outside Opinions

Some freedom fails

because of perfectly executed

consideration.

You Don't Fight Alone

There's this quiet misconception that everyone else somehow has life better under control.

That they get through things more easily. Doubt less. Carry less.

And then you meet. Talk a bit more honestly. And realize:

Everyone is carrying something.

Different packages.

Different weights.

Different levels of visibility.

Some you notice right away. Others only when someone has the courage to talk about them.

And that's where something important happens:

The loneliness gets quieter.

Not because the problems disappear. But because you realize:

I'm not strange.

I'm not weak.

I'm not the only one.

Sharing isn't complaining.

It's relief.

And asking for help isn't a sign of failure.

It's a sign that you take yourself seriously.

Packages

Everyone carries something.

Some of it you can see.

Some of it you can't.

Comparing Without Making Yourself Smaller

Comparison happens.

Whether you want it to or not.

You see others and think:

"They can still do that."

"They have it easier."

Or sometimes: "At least I'm better off there."

The difference isn't in comparing itself.

It's in where your gaze goes.

Comparison can make you feel smaller.

Or grateful.

You can see what you've lost.

Or what's still there.

Often, both are true at the same time. And it's no shame to admit:

I can't do some things anymore.

But I might do other things better.

Or more calmly.

Or more consciously.

Seeing the positive doesn't mean denying what's difficult.

It just means you don't look downward exclusively.

Perspective

Comparison can weigh you down.

Or it can carry you.

The direction of your gaze decides.

Accepting Different Paths

You know your path.

Work.

Security.

Responsibility.

It worked. So it becomes the benchmark.

When someone chooses a different path, it can seem unreasonable at first.

Unstable.

Maybe even a little naïve.

You mean well.

And you start explaining — just in case — why your model has proven itself.

Only later does it sink in that "proven" isn't a quality seal for everyone.

It's just an experience.

Paths

Experience knows a lot.

But it doesn't know everything.

Lonely Is Not the Same as Being Alone

Loneliness is a quiet feeling.

It doesn't make noise. It simply sits down beside you.

You can be surrounded by people and still feel lonely. And you can be alone and still feel connected.

That's what makes it so difficult — and so human.

Over the years, our surroundings often change.

People leave.

Relationships shift.

Roles dissolve.

Children build their own lives. Friends move away or grow quieter. Things that once felt natural are suddenly no longer there.

And then this thought appears: "Am I alone now?"

Maybe the more honest question is a different one: "Who am I actually still truly connected to?"

Loneliness doesn't mean you've failed. It often just means that something has changed and the old ways no longer hold.

What helps is rarely frantic action. Not immediately doing "more." Not immediately trying to "function."

What helps is awareness.

Noticing:

I need closeness right now.

Or conversation.

Or simply someone who's there — without offering solutions.

And sometimes, admitting that to yourself is already a big step.

Loneliness loses its sharpness when you stop seeing it as a flaw and start understanding it as a signal.

Not as an accusation.

But as an invitation.

Closeness

*Loneliness doesn't mean
that no one is there.*

*Sometimes it simply means
that you want to be seen.*

Letting Go Is Not a Devaluation

Letting go often sounds bigger than it actually feels.

You imagine goodbyes. Final cuts. That cold feeling of "no longer being needed."

But most of the time, letting go is much quieter.

It happens when children start living their own lives.

When closeness changes.

When roles that once mattered are no longer required.

And yes — that can be frightening.

The fear of being less important.

The fear of losing your place.

The fear that love will shrink if it's no longer confirmed every day.

But love doesn't work like ownership.

It doesn't get smaller just because it moves on.

Sometimes it even grows when you stop holding on so tightly.

Letting go doesn't mean you stop mattering.

It means you trust.

You trust that everyone is allowed to find their own path. And that closeness doesn't disappear just because it looks different.

Maybe this is one of the most demanding tasks of growing older:

Not holding on where you once held tightly.

And still being there.

Open.

Kind.

Without demands.

That's not withdrawal.

That's maturity.

Trust

Love needs closeness.

But it also needs space.

Both are allowed to exist at the same time.

Sweets & Quietly Undermining the Parenting

You want to do it right.

Really right.

You watch sugar, habits, long-term effects that might be lurking somewhere between a chocolate bar and adult life.

You're consistent. Exemplary, even.

With your own parents' voices in your head, explaining that you have to be careful.

So you are.

Very.

Years later, you're sitting together calmly, and a now-older child casually mentions:

"Oh, at Grandma and Grandpa's we always got sweets."

Always is not a casual word.

It gets checked.

Confirmed.

With a matter-of-factness that leaves no room for doubt.

When you ask about it, the explanation comes without hesitation:

With grandchildren, you do things differently.

And when they're there, they're allowed to have it.

You nod.

And realize that parenting principles apparently change their validity based on the child's date of birth.

And that it's surprisingly hard to stay consistent when someone in the background is generously working against you.

Right ... or Not?

"Right" is sometimes just what fits the role.

Parents are consistent.

Grandparents are generous.

Children remember the opening hours.

Acceptance Is Not Giving Up

Acceptance has an image problem.

Many people confuse it with resignation.

With "Well, that's just how it is."

With a shrug.

With an internal retreat.

But acceptance is something else entirely.

Acceptance doesn't mean that you like something.

It only means that you stop fighting reality.

You can be sad and still accept.

You can be angry and still acknowledge that something is the way it is right now.

Acceptance is the moment when the energy you used to spend on resisting becomes available to you again.

Not to sugarcoat anything.

But to move forward.

Because only when you stop saying, "This shouldn't be happening," is there space for the question:

"What do I need now?"

Acceptance isn't an ending.

It's a beginning without resistance.

Reality

Acceptance doesn't mean that you like something.

It just means you stop wearing yourself down on it.

Gentleness Is When You Stop Yelling at Yourself

You used to be hard on yourself. Very hard.

You'd snap at yourself internally when something didn't work. You pushed yourself, compared yourself, pulled yourself together.

At some point, you realize:

That takes more energy than it gives back.

Gentleness is not carelessness.

Gentleness is experience.

Gentleness is the moment when you realize:

"I don't have to parent myself anymore."

When something goes wrong, you no longer say:

"How stupid can you be?"

You say something more like:

"Ah. One of those days again."

You learn to listen to yourself instead of correcting yourself.

And surprisingly, after that, many things work better.

Not faster.

But more calmly.

Maybe gentleness is the thing you once wished someone had given you — and that you're finally giving yourself now.

Gentleness

You're allowed to be kind to yourself.

After all, you'll be living with yourself for quite a while.

The Role You Mistake for Your Face

People like to say, "With age comes ease. As we grow older, we become more ourselves."

A lovely story.

Sometimes it's true. Often it isn't.

Something else often happens instead: roles harden. Not because people become cruel — but because routine starts to feel like identity. The longer you do something, the more you begin to believe: This is who I am.

The provider.

The strong one.

The independent one.

The reasonable one.

The one who needs nothing.

The one who always functions.

These aren't just quirks. They are survival systems.

And they are trained so well that we mistake them for character.

That's why this scene from the video strikes me so deeply:

These people are walking in their public mode. Everything in place. Everything controlled. Everything "normal."

And then — a glance, a person, a moment of recognition — and suddenly something falls away that seemed permanently attached.

Not because someone "makes them better."

But because someone makes them safe.

And then I think: maybe this is the kind of nonsense we're never too old for.

The idea that we are only the role.

That we must always function.

That we manage ourselves instead of living.

Maybe maturity isn't: "I have myself under control."

Maybe maturity is: "I know when I'm playing a part — and I know how to find my way back."

Back to a gaze that is allowed to soften.

Back to a laugh that doesn't need justification.

Back to a body that doesn't carry constant tension just to survive in the world.

And if you're truly honest:

Some people don't become more authentic with age.

They simply become more professional at functioning.

Authenticity doesn't arrive automatically.

It arrives when you remember what you feel like without the mask.

This isn't about youth.

It isn't about romance.

It's about being human.

And sometimes all it takes is a single moment — when you see someone, and your entire system says:

There. Home.

The Role

*Routine eventually begins to
feel like identity.*

*But not every strength is your
true nature.*

*Sometimes all it takes is a safe,
steady gaze,*

*and something falls away that
was never your face.*

We Might Need Diapers Again One Day

I had a dream that I had wet my pants.

Not symbolically.

Not in some poetic, mysterious way.

Very literally.

In the dream, it was one of those unmistakable moments of total loss of control. That quiet inner panic. That immediate: Oh no. Please no.

And as happens with dreams like this, I half woke up. Not fully conscious.

But awake enough to think: Please let this not be real.

Carefully, very carefully, I checked the bed. Slowly. Methodically. Like someone conducting a highly sensitive inspection of personal dignity.

Relief. Everything dry. Civilization intact.

In the morning, I told my husband.

"I dreamed I wet my pants."

He listened.

Then I added, completely calmly with knowing grin:

"Well... one day we'll need diapers again anyway."

I didn't say it dramatically. It was more of a practical reflection on the circle of life.

We begin in diapers.

We gain independence.

And perhaps, someday, we return.

He reacted instantly shocked.

"Let's slow down. Easy."

His expression said it all:

We are not there. We are still fine. No need to jump to the final chapter just yet.

I, however, had already moved into a quiet, humorous acceptance of biology.

Not fearful. Not tragic. Just aware.

Because the body has its own language. Sometimes it sends reminders in the night. Small simulations. Gentle warnings.

First diapers. Then freedom. And maybe, one day, diapers again.

The bed was dry.

Our dignity preserved.

Our relationship solid.

And my husband would very much prefer that no preparations be made at this time.

The body may rehearse the future.

But for now, we are still comfortably in the middle of the story.

Loss of Control

Cosmos in a flesh suit with a built-in alarm system.

A nighttime rehearsal of losing control.

Morning mattress inspection with full seriousness.

Still stable. Still independent. Humor intact.

The Circle Closes

Sometimes growing older feels like the circle is closing.

You slow down again.

You need more help again.

At times, you feel more helpless again.

And yes — that can hurt.

And still, there's something many people understand only very late:

It's a privilege to experience the entire cycle.

Not because everything is beautiful.

But because it means: I'm still here.

Many don't get that chance.

They're taken out of life halfway through — without closure, without that quiet ripening.

And that softens your gaze:

Not everything has to feel good to be real.

Every phase asks us to accept it.

Not as a reward.

Not as "meaning."

But as an opportunity to grow inward once more.

The circle closes.

And sometimes there's a quiet dignity in exactly that.

We Keep Circling

Some things come back.

Not as an ending — more like:

"Ah, I know this."

And then it continues — with
more experience

and less drama.

What I Simply Leave Behind Today

There are things I used to take very seriously.

Too seriously.

Discussions where no one was listening.

Opinions no one wanted to change.

Explanations no one actually needed.

Today, I leave those behind.

I leave discussions that are only about winning.

I leave the need to be right when it costs more energy than it gives.

I leave people who constantly want to correct me but never listen themselves.

I leave perfection. It was never reachable anyway and brought me surprisingly little joy.

And above all, I leave one thing behind: making myself small because I do things differently than I used to.

I move more slowly.

I plan more generously.

I take breaks seriously.

And sometimes, I don't take myself quite so seriously anymore.

This isn't retreat.

It's choice.

And choice is a luxury.

Choice

You can't hold on to everything.

But you can choose what you carry.

I Take the Elevator

I used to take the stairs.

Not because they were nicer. But because that's just what you do.

Today I stand there with a choice. Stairs or elevator. And I think: "Elevator."

Not out of laziness.

Not out of defiance.

But because my knee and my ambition are currently holding very different opinions.

And that's new:

I don't argue anymore.

I don't explain myself.

I take the elevator.

It doesn't feel like giving up.

It feels like coordination.

With myself.

Sometimes the body needs a detour.

And sometimes the detour is simply the better route.

Making the Path Easier

I take the elevator.

Not out of convenience.

Out of experience.

I Take a Break

There are days when everything flows.

And days when nothing does.

In the past, I would have pushed through.

Teeth clenched. Keep going. Move on.

Today, I notice sooner:

"I'm taking a break now."

Not because I can't.

But because I can.

A break isn't a standstill.

A break is maintenance.

And maintenance makes sure

you can continue afterward.

Pause

I take a break.

Not because I'm giving up.

Because life needs maintenance.

A Small Realization (Without Much Fuss)

Detours and pauses aren't failure.

They're adjustment with experience.

You don't have to accomplish everything.

You're allowed to choose wisely.

Let's Just Play

You're sitting at the table.

A game is ready. The instructions get read.

Once.

Twice.

And then someone carefully says:

"Um ... does anyone actually understand this?"

Everyone looks around. No one says anything. The silence becomes suspicious.

And at some point it's clear:

No.

No one understands it.

Not really.

Not confidently enough to explain how this is actually supposed to work.

And that's where it gets interesting.

Cards are played.

Dice are rolled.

Rules are invented that feel logical in the moment.

They're adjusted along the way.

There's a brief discussion — and then laughter.

At some point, no one remembers what was originally intended and what was improvised on the spot.

But everyone's in.

Everyone's playing.

And everyone's having fun.

Sometimes chaos isn't the problem. It's the solution.

And honestly:

This version of the game is often funnier and more alive than anything the instructions ever promised.

Rules of the Game

When no one understands the instructions,

everyone invents new rules together.

And suddenly,

life becomes a lot more fun.

Wings Beneath the Cloth

When babies sleep, they are often swaddled.

The cloth wraps snugly around their bodies, holding their arms close, limiting their movement.

It looks like restriction. But it is safety.

Tightness means security.

Containment means comfort.

Their tiny bodies know this. They remember the space they came from.

And then the cloth is opened.

Slowly.

Gently.

And suddenly something happens that touches the heart every time:

The arms lift.

The fingers spread.

The whole body stretches into the world.

It looks as if a small angel is unfolding its wings.

No hesitation.

No self-consciousness.

No "Am I allowed?"

Just movement.

Just expansion.

Just being.

Perhaps we all carry this memory within us.

The knowing of what it feels like to be held — and the knowing of what it feels like to unfold.

Protection is not the enemy.

It is preparation.

But it is not the destination.

There comes a moment when we are meant to lift our arms. To stretch without explanation. To take up space without apology.

Maybe maturity is not about needing no armor.

Maybe maturity is about knowing when to open it.

We were all once beings with invisible wings.

And sometimes a single safe moment is enough for them to remember.

Opening

What looks like limitation was once protection.

Safety is not a cage, but preparation.

Maturity does not mean living without a shell.

Maturity means knowing when to open it.

Is Age a Crazy Thing?

Sometimes it's not life that's acting strange.

Not technology.

Not even the world.

Sometimes it's just age.

It forgets things.

Mixes up processes.

And likes to chime in without being asked.

But it's not crazy in a malicious way.

More ... creatively.

It blends experience with fatigue.

Wisdom with confusion.

And builds situations out of them that you might once have shaken your head at — and now laugh about wholeheartedly.

Maybe age isn't working against us.

Maybe it's working with us.

And honestly:

If you can still laugh about it,

a surprising amount is going right.

Age Is a Crazy Thing

Sometimes age gets a little weird.

But it's not personal.

It's just checking
whether you can still laugh.

Too Old for This Nonsense?

The honest answer is: It depends.

Too old for drama?

Yes.

Too old for unnecessary stress?

Hopefully.

Too old for nonsense?

Absolutely not.

Maybe nonsense is exactly the thing you should protect the longest.

Not as an escape. But as a reminder that life isn't working against you.

It stumbles sometimes.

It creaks.

It asks stupid questions.

And every now and then it presses the wrong button.

And us?

We laugh.

Shake our heads.

And keep going.

With detours.

With gentleness.

With humor.

And if someone asks whether you're not a bit too old for that by now:

Nonsense.

You Get Older.

But you don't lose your sense
of humor.

That would truly be a shame.